CAN'T SLEEP

Chris Raschka

ORCHARD BOOKS NEW YORK

Orchard Books, 95 Madison Avenue, New York, NY 10016

Manufactured in the United States of America. Printed by Barton Press, Inc.
Bound by Horowitz/Rae. Book design by Mina Greenstein. The text of this book is set in 24 point Korinna.
The illustrations are watercolor paintings reproduced in full color.   10   9   8   7   6   5   4   3   2   1

Library of Congress Cataloging-in-Publication Data
Raschka, Christopher. Can't sleep / Chris Raschka.   p.   cm.
"A Richard Jackson book"—Half t.p. Summary: The moon comforts bedtime fears.
ISBN 0-531-09479-0.   ISBN 0-531-08779-4 (lib. bdg.)
[1. Dogs—Fiction. 2. Moon—Fiction. 3. Bedtime—Fiction. 4. Sleep—Fiction. 5. Fear—Fiction.
6. Stories in rhyme.]   I. Title.   PZ8.3.R177Can   1995   [E]—dc20   94-48805

RASCHKA

For Paul and Renate

When you can't sleep
the moon will keep

you safe. The moon
will stay awake.

When your big brother
goes to bed

and sleeps
and you can't sleep,

the moon will watch
you in your room.

When you can't sleep
and you now hear

your mother moving
in the hall,

in the bathroom
washing up, and

closing her door

the moon will rise
and see you in

your bed and see
your open eyes.

When you can't sleep   your father turning
when you now hear   off the lights

and walking down
the hall and shutting
that door tight,

the moon will hear,
the moon will hear
this too.

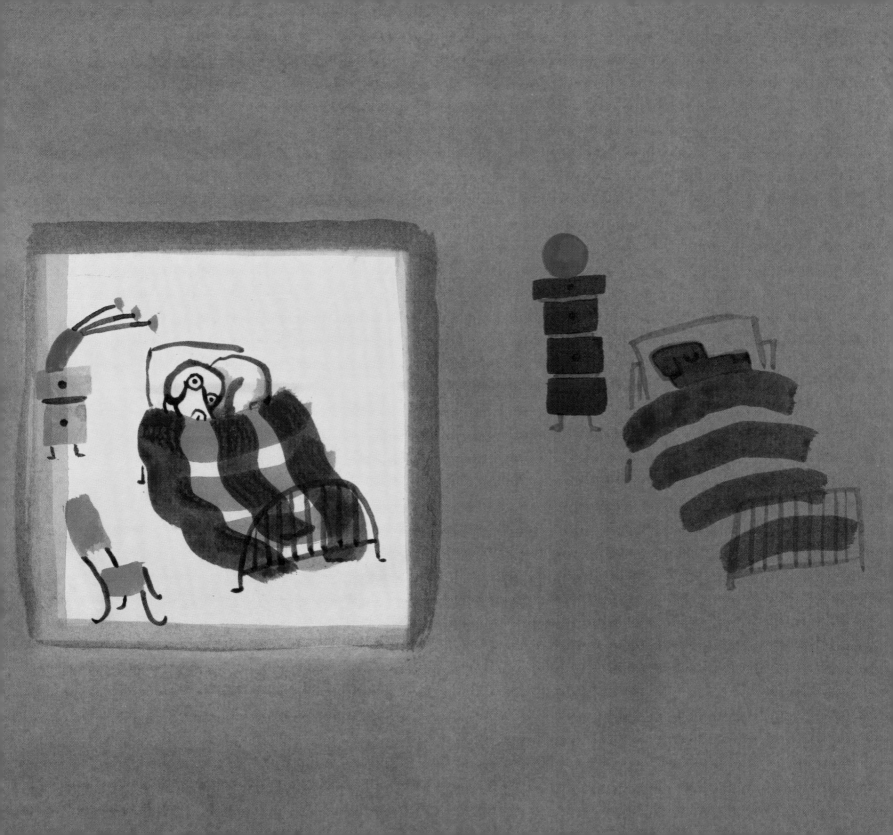

Now when there is
no sound

the moon can tell
you feel frightened
and are lonely.

The moon will stay
awake for you.

The moon will stay
awake for you
until you too
are sleeping.

The moon will stay
awake for you
until you too
are sleeping.

When morning comes

the moon will go

to bed. Now you   may stay awake

and keep her safe . . .

you'll keep her safe.